In memory of Michaela Mabinty DePrince—
a trailblazer and treasure to all who
encountered her light, and her life.
With many thanks to the entire editorial
team who worked on this book.
—L.O.

For my dear mum, Edna Ifeagwu.
And for Claire, Alyson, Rachel, and Karina—
I'll love ballet for life because of this book!
—O.D.

Becoming a Ballerina: The Story of Michaela Mabinty DePrince
Text copyright © 2025 by Laura Obuobi
Illustrations copyright © 2025 by Olivia Duchess
All rights reserved. Manufactured in Italy.
No part of this book may be used or reproduced in any manner whatsoever without written permission
except in the case of brief quotations embodied in critical articles and reviews. For information address
HarperCollins Children's Books, a division of HarperCollins Publishers, 195 Broadway, New York, NY 10007.
www.harpercollinschildrens.com

Library of Congress Control Number: 2024940300
ISBN 978-0-06-322246-5

The artist used Procreate to create the digital illustrations for this book.
Typography by Rachel Zegar
24 25 26 27 28 RTLO 10 9 8 7 6 5 4 3 2 1

First Edition

Becoming a Ballerina

The Story of Michaela Mabinty DePrince

Written by **Laura Obuobi**   Illustrated by **Olivia Duchess**

HARPER
An Imprint of HarperCollinsPublishers

It begins during a dust storm in a small town in Sierra Leone. Inside an orphanage, a little girl named Mabinty listens to the wind swish and swoosh, while her heart cries for her mother and father.

The wind whistles in a voice that tugs on Mabinty's feet. She rises.

But in the storm, all Mabinty sees is the whirling, dusty wind.

All she feels is a dry hole in her heart.

And then . . . the wind dances a magazine into her sight

and into her outstretched hand.

Mabinty gazes at the cover. The dancer smiles a ribbon of hope around Mabinty's heart.

Ballet begins to pulse joy all the way from Mabinty's heart to the crown of her head and down to the tips of her toes.

Sometime later, Mabinty and the other children are readied for adoption. Everyone gets a book with pictures of their new families—

everyone, except Mabinty.

Mabinty wishes for a family who won't care about the white spots on her skin.

Most of all, Mabinty wishes to live with her friend and her friend's new family.

Every night, the dancer's smile whispers hope and the promise of a better life one day.

Every night, the wind breathes life into the promise and into Mabinty's wishes. It begins to take shape when . . .

. . . she and her friend become sisters, in the bosom of their new mother.

With a new name, Michaela is swooped into the United States, into a home swirling with love,

and before long, Michaela twirls into . . .

. . . ballet class.

Her heels kiss.

Her knees bend.

Her arms float up like a swan, reaching for the sky.

Michaela shimmies into a
tutu for her first show

but turns away from her
reflection in the mirror.

"Can I become a ballerina with my spots?"
"Yes, you can become a ballerina with your spots."

Ballet pulses faith all the way from her heart
to the crown of her head and down to the tips of
her toes.

On that first stage, Michaela is triumphant.
She sautés with poise and jetés with grace.

Michaela immerses herself in the ballet world, reading magazines, watching performances.

But . . . she longs to see girls with all shades of brown skin onstage.

Michaela paints her pointe shoes.

Her mother dyes her tights.

She wants to feel like herself onstage. She wants her
movements to reach all the way to her toes and fingertips,
like the other ballerinas' when they perform.

"Can a girl with *my* brown skin
become a ballerina?"
"Yes, a girl with your brown
skin can become a ballerina."

Still, her question weighs her down.
Yet . . .

. . . ballet pulses strength all the way from her heart to the crown of her head and down to the tips of her toes. Michaela rises, glissés and chaînés with poise, and arabesques with grace.

Michaela embraces the ballet world . . .

. . . but the ballet world doesn't embrace her back.

"She doesn't have the right body for ballet."

"She's not soft or delicate . . . she's too muscular."

"It's better if everyone looks the same."

"Shouldn't you dance jazz
or hip-hop?"

Their words are
an angry cacophony
threatening to unravel
the ribbon of hope
around her heart.

Their words are an angry cacophony that crushes her spirit.

"Will I ever become a ballerina?"
"Yes, you will become a ballerina. Don't let their words
bury your joy or the gift inside you."

Michaela dries her face and rises again.

She holds her head up and pirouettes into . . .

a beloved princess.

Grand jetés into . . .

a dainty fairy.

And fouettés into . . .

an enchanting swan.

On that big stage, Michaela soars.
Ballet is the gift that pulses all the way from her heart to
the crown of her head and down to the tips of her toes.

She is a breath of light,
stirring joy and faith into anyone with a dream,
whispering strength into every dancer's soul, and
twirling ribbons of hope around hearts—little girls with brown skin
who want to become ballerinas like Michaela Mabinty DePrince.

Author's Note

When I was little, I liked to stand on my tippy toes. (Truth is, as a grown-up, I still stand on my tippy toes sometimes—it feels really good!) An uncle of mine would always laugh when he saw me do this and ask, "You want to be a ballerina when you grow up, don't you?" I never became a ballerina—I preferred getting happily lost in stories instead. I still love stories and, a few years ago, I found myself happily lost in the story of ballerina Michaela Mabinty DePrince.

Michaela DePrince was born Mabinty Bangura in Sierra Leone but lost her birth parents when she was three years old to the civil war happening there. Soon after, she was taken to an orphanage where she was abused because of her vitiligo. Vitiligo is when the skin loses its color and begins to turn pale and white in patches. Anyone can have vitiligo, but it is most obvious on people with brown skin. Michaela had a very difficult experience at the orphanage, but she also had a best friend (her sister, Mia Mabinty DePrince), who made her feel safe and loved.

Michaela, like many Black ballerinas, often endured hurtful comments and questions about whether she belonged in the ballet world, even while she nurtured her love for classical ballet. Michaela's parents, Elaine and Charles DePrince, showered her with support as her mentors, and her own perseverance helped her push through these challenges to become one of the world's premier ballerinas. Like many brown-skinned ballerinas intent on perfecting their skill, she advocated for dancing in tights and pointe shoes that matched her skin tone whenever she could. Unlike with brown tights, it was only in 2017 that one dancewear company began selling brown pointe shoes; other dancewear companies finally joined in in 2020. That meant that for a long time, ballerinas with brown skin had to paint their pointe shoes, usually with makeup, to match their skin tone. Yet, despite this change in the industry, some ballerinas continue to paint their shoes because a wider spectrum of brown tones for pointe shoes is still needed. This is also where the question of belonging is evident—very few dancers of color, particularly dark-skinned dancers, are hired into predominantly white classical ballet companies.

Michaela DePrince's determination to push through prejudice and racism and succeed in the classical ballet world was affirming and inspiring. And her place in the classical ballet world gave permission to all Black girls to perceive themselves as premier ballerinas. Michaela died on September 10, 2024, leaving a legacy of passion and gracefulness that reminds everyone of the beauty we all get to experience when our world is meaningfully inclusive.

Selected Sources

BOOKS

Copeland, Misty. *Black Ballerinas: My Journey to Our Legacy*. New York: Simon and Schuster, 2021.

DePrince, Elaine, and Michaela DePrince. *Taking Flight: From War Orphan to Star Ballerina*. New York: Ember, an imprint of Random House Children's Books, 2014.

FILMS

Kargman, Bess, dir. *First Position*, 2011; Los Angeles, CA: First Position Films, 2012. HD, 94 minutes.

WQED Digital Docs, "En Pointe: Black Dancers, Black History." Aired February 28, 2020, on WQED. www.pbs.org/video/en-pointe-black-dancers-black-history-jnjddv.

MAGAZINE AND NEWSPAPER ARTICLES

Adesina, Precious. "At Ballet Black, Creating Opportunity for British Dancers." *New York Times*. Updated May 12, 2022. www.nytimes.com/2022/04/25/arts/dance/ballet-black-london.html.

Brown, Stacia L. "Where Are the black ballerinas?" *Washington Post*. May 5, 2014. www.washingtonpost.com/news/act-four/wp/2014/05/05/where-are-the-black-ballerinas.

Howard, Theresa Ruth. "Michaela DePrince Makes Her Next Move." *Pointe*. November 3, 2021. www.pointemagazine.com/michaela-deprince.

Lansky, Chava Pearl. "Six Major Dancewear Brands Announce Plans to Release Pointe Shoes in Diverse Shades." *Pointe*. Updated June 12, 2020. www.pointemagazine.com/bloch-pointe-shoes-diverse-shades.

Marshall, Alex. "Brown Point Shoes Arrive, 200 Years after White Ones." *New York Times*. November 4, 2018. www.nytimes.com/2018/11/04/arts/dance/brown-point-shoes-diversity-ballet.html.

WEBSITES AND ONLINE MEDIA

DePrince, Michaela. michaeladeprince.com.

Goodman-Hughey, Ericka N. "Michaela DePrince on Her Journey from War Orphan in Sierra Leone to World-Class Ballerina." ESPN. February 13, 2019. www.espn.com/espnw/culture/story/_/id/25984750/michaela-deprince-journey-war-orphan-sierra-leone-world-class-ballerina.

Kelly, Megyn. "Against All Odds. Ballerina Michaela DePrince's Remarkable Journey." NBC News. July 16, 2017. www.nbcnews.com/video/against-all-odds-ballerina-michaela-deprince-s-remarkable-journey-1001306691596.

Stump, Scott. "Popular Dance Shoe Companies Vow to Make Ballet Shoes for Dancers of Color." *Today*. Updated June 11, 2020. www.today.com/style/brown-ballet-shoes-are-making-dancers-color-feel-welcomed-accepted-t151656.